For Alex (who is also a star)

PUFFIN BOOKS
Published by the Penguin Group: London, New York,
Australia, Canada, India, Ireland, New Zealand and South Africa
Penguin Books Ltd, Registered Offices:
80 Strand, London WC2R 0RL, England

penguin.com

First published 2007
1 3 5 7 9 10 8 6 4 2
Copyright © Michael Broad, 2007
All rights reserved
The moral right of the author/illustrator has been asserted
Printed in China
ISBN 978-0-141-50122-2

The Little Star who Wished

Michael Broad

PUFFIN

One dark night, high above the world,
a little star lay dreaming.
He dreamed he was a comet,
blazing across the sky, when suddenly . . . the
little star
began
to
fall.

Down,
down
he fell
and the children
who saw him
made a wish
upon a
falling
star.

Holding
his
teddy
tight,
the little
star
tumbled

on
and on
until . . .

SPLASH!

They both plunged deep into the sea.

As the little star sank down towards the seabed, he looked all around. He couldn't believe what he saw – strange creatures in all shapes and sizes.

They were stripy and spotty, spiky and wobbly. But none of them were starry.

The little star held his teddy tight.
The night sky seemed far, far away.

Then he saw tiny lights twinkling in the distance.
"Stars!" he cried, and his heart
filled with joy.

But when he got closer, he saw
that they were not stars at all.
Just curious creatures that
glowed and glistened.

"There are no other stars
    down here, Teddy,"
said the little star as
                he sat on a rock.
    "I want to go home."

"Don't cry," said the rock,
    which was not a rock at all,
but a turtle. "There are lots
            of stars in the ocean."

"Stars like me?"
The little star brightened.
"But where are they?"

"In the starship," said the turtle.
"Hold on tight – I'll take you there."

They swooshed through the water, past the dogfish out for a walk and the catfish on the prowl....

past the stripy zebra fish and a family of seahorses.

And **on** and **on** they swam,
deeper and **deeper**,
until there on the seabed
they found an old shipwreck
glowing with light.
"The starship!"
gasped the little star.

They peered inside. There, looking up
at the little star, were lots of starfish.

"But they're not quite the
same as me," he whispered.
"I shine brightly in the night sky
and grant wishes."

"There are lots of stars in the world," a wise old starfish said. "Stars of the sky and stars of the sea. Starfish have a little magic too – we grant wishes for all those who live beneath the waves."

The little star climbed to the very
top of the shipwreck and looked
longingly upwards.

He remembered
the twinkling
brightness of the
night sky, the comets
with their fiery tails.
"Everyone is very kind,"
said the little star,
"but I would really
like to go home."

Suddenly he had an idea.
"I'll build a ladder!
A ladder tall enough to reach the sky.
I can climb all the way home."

"Then we will help you,"
the starfish said.

So they all set to work,
helping the little star
make his way home.

up . . .
up,
Up,

the
ladder
began
to
grow.

The
little star
and his
teddy
climbed
higher

and

higher . . .

. . . but the ladder was too short.

"I'll never shine in
the night sky again,"
said the little star sadly.

The wise old starfish thought for a moment.
"All stars have star-magic to grant wishes,"
he said, "so perhaps we can help you.
Perhaps it's time for you to make a wish."

The stars of the sea gathered
around the little star of the sky
as he closed his eyes and
wished with all his heart until . . .

Whooooosh!

The little star shot up
into the sky just
like a fiery comet.

"Oh, thank you!"
he cried. "Wishes **do** come true,
even for little stars
like me!"

That night, and every night thereafter,
the little star shone down on the
world below, looking out
for special wishes.

And if you look
    very carefully,
  you might just see
the little star whose
      very own wish
        came true.